THE BIGGEST
She's Ever Had

HOT EROTICA

JUST PLAIN BOB

WARNING

This book contains sexually explicit scenes and adult language. It may be considered offensive to some readers. This book is for sale to adults ONLY.

* * * * * * * * * * * * * * * * * *

Please store your files wisely where they cannot be accessed by underage readers.

Please feel free to send me an email. Just know that these emails are filtered by my publisher. Good news is always welcome.

Just Plain Bob - **justplainbob@awesomeauthors.org**

About the Publisher

4Fun Publishing, a member of **BLVNP Incorporated**, 340 S. Lemon #6200, Walnut CA 91789, info@blvnp.com / legal@blvnp.com
NOTE: Due to the highly emotional reaction of some people to works of erotic fiction, any email sent to the above address that contains foul language or religious references is automatically deleted by our anti-spam software and will not be seen. All other communications are welcome.

DISCLAIMER

Please don't be stupid and kill yourself. This book is a work of FICTION. Do not try any new sexual practice that you find in this book. It is fiction and not to be confused with reality. Neither the author nor the publisher or its associates assume any responsibility for any loss, injury, death or legal consequences resulting from acting on the contents in this book. Every character in this book is over 18 years of age. The author's opinions are not to be construed as the opinions of the publisher. The material in this book is for entertainment purposes ONLY. Enjoy.

The Biggest She's Ever Had

Hot Erotica

By: Just Plain Bob

© **Just Plain Bob 2015**
ISBN: 978-1-68030-311-7

Two months ago if anyone had told me I'd get a kick out of watching another man put it to my wife I'd have suggested that they be committed. I just watched Kathy spend two hours trying to fuck a guy I don't even know to death, and she damn near did it. He was decidedly weak in the knees when he staggered out to go home and, as a matter of fact, so was I. It was only the back wall of the closet that was holding me up. It all came about as the result of a simple question, one that I ask every year, although this year's answer was nowhere near what I expected.

***

"Honey, what do you want for your birthday?"

Kathy thought for a minute and then said, "Honestly? Promise you won't get mad?"

What the hell kind of question is that I thought, all I want to know is what kind of present to get her, and she wants me to promise I won't get mad? "Why should I get mad? If you want it and I can get it, I will."

Several moments of silence and then she said, "Don't take this wrong Jimmy, you know I love you to death, but what I'm going to say is so off the wall that you have to promise me you won't get mad."

It was obvious to me that she wasn't going to tell me unless I promised and so I did.

"Honey," she said, "I want to experience a really big cock."

My jaw damn near hit the floor. Kathy saw the expression on my face and she hastened to say, "Baby, it's not what you think. I'm not unhappy with you, I'm just curious."

After I recovered enough to be coherent she explained to me the reason for her request. Kathy plays bridge every Thursday night with some friends of hers from college, and it always turns out that the evening's main topic, after all the gossip is dished out, is sex. The discussion on sex always seems to concentrate in two areas, oral sex, both giving and getting, and cock size. The talk on oral sex covered like and dislikes, techniques, who was good at it and who wasn't. But where the talk on oral sex was general in nature, the talk on cock size was much more specific. It covered things like length, girth, coloring, texture (I didn't even know that a cock had texture), shape, bends and whether or not it was circumcised. Four of the girls had experienced what they considered to be large cocks, and of the four one was married to a guy who had a large dick and one was going steady with a guy who was extremely large. The debate constantly raged between the eight girls as to which was better, size alone or knowing how to use it. Four of the girls, the ones who hadn't had a large cock, said that if a guy knew how to make love to a woman size didn't matter. The other four, the ones who had tried a larger than average cock, said that even if a guy wasn't a good lover, if he had a big dick he could still satisfy a girl better than a guy with a smaller dick who knew how to use it. The debate had raged for years and finally Kathy's curiosity had gotten to the point where she wanted to find out for herself.

"Well?" she asked when she had finished talking.

I didn't answer right away; I was still in shock. Finally I said, "Well, that's a bit of a surprise and I don't know what to say. I'm going to have to think on that for a while."

***

Basically I'm a pretty secure guy. I'm comfortable in my maleness or manliness or whatever you want to call it and I was not concerned that some guy with a big cock would steal Kathy away from me. I was pretty sure that Kathy loved me enough to stay around, and her being with another man, while not something to fill my heart with joy, was something I already knew I could handle. During the early years of our marriage Kathy had gone through several affairs and I'd found out about them. She doesn't know that I know about them and I've always figured that it was my fault anyway. Kathy is a sex maniac in bed and I was spending all my time trying to establish my career and I neglected to take care of business at home. As soon as I started taking care of my husbandly obligations she quit having affairs and for the past fourteen years or so she has been faithful to me, at least as far as I know.

What I did know was that Kathy wasn't asking me to find her a stud, no, she already had one in mind, and all she was asking me for was my blessing. What would happen if I said no? Since she probably already had someone in mind would she go ahead and do it anyway, and hide it from me? After giving the matter a great deal of thought I decided, "better the devil you know than the devil you don't" and I told Kathy that she could have what she wanted for her birthday. She threw her arms around me and kissed me and told me I was the best husband ever and that she loved me and that I wouldn't be sorry and yadda yadda yadda.

"So what's the plan?" I asked. "You going out for the night or should I get a hotel room for the night?"

Kathy chuckled and said, "No way baby. I want you right next to me holding my hand."

For the second time my jaw almost hit the floor and I stood there looking at her and feeling like an idiot. I hadn't expected that and I was at a loss for words. Finally I stammered that I didn't think that I could do that.

"I don't think that I could watch you do another man. It's going to be hard enough on me just knowing that you're doing it."

Kathy pleaded with me and listed all the reasons why she wanted me there, the most important of them being, "What if he's too big and I can't take him without a lot of pain and he won't stop once he's started?"

I finally agreed to be near, if not right in the room with her, close enough to hear her if she hollered for help. I was right, she did have her stud already picked out. He was a male dancer at one of the local topless bars that had special "women's only" nights twice a week. He'd come recommended by one of her bridge club friends. The plan was for him to show up at Kathy's birthday party and do a Happy Birthday strip-o-gram. He did not know that the party was going to be just him and Kathy. The plan we eventually settled on (with a great deal of reluctance on my part) was that I would be in the downstairs den when he arrived so that I could be close if things went bad right from the start. If things went well initially Kathy would take him to the bedroom and when they were inside I would go upstairs and be in the guest bedroom, close enough to hear her cry for help if she had to. The closer we got to Kathy's birthday the less I cared for the plan. For one thing, if I was close enough to hear her cry for help, I'd also be close enough to hear what was going on and I really, really didn't want that. But every attempt to back out was met with a "You promised" and so I was stuck with going through with it.

***

The big day arrived and I was a fucking basket case. I might as well have skipped work that day for all that I accomplished. When I got home Kathy had dinner ready - all my favorites - but I couldn't eat a thing. I had a couple of belts of Wild Turkey to try and calm my nerves, but Kathy took the bottle away from me, "I don't want you passed out if I have to holler for help. I'll help you settle down," and she walked me into the den, sat me down in the desk chair, and gave me head. She was right; it did settle me right down, right up to the point where the doorbell rang. Kathy got up and tucked me in and said, "Later lover," and went to answer the door. I kept the door closed until I heard the stripper's boom box start to play and then I opened the door a crack and peeked out. Kathy was sitting in one of the straight backed dining room chairs and the stripper was doing his dance for her; so far no problems and I went back to the desk and picked up a book that I had been in the middle of. After a couple of minutes trying to read it was obvious to me that I wasn't going to be able to concentrate, not with what was going on in the other room. I went back to the door and cracked it open and took a look.

Until then I don't believe I had ever been envious of someone else or insecure, but what I saw when I opened that door made me feel both. The dancer had a cock on him that would have made a horse proud. It was just over eleven inches long (Kathy measured it) and was as big around as a summer sausage. It was rock hard and bobbing back and forth about an inch away from Kathy's face and her eyes were locked on it in rapt fascination. As I watched, one of her hands came up and I saw a finger touch his cockhead and then trace a circle around it. Then the hand came up and encircled the cock and the dancer began to move, fucking Kathy's fist. Her other hand took hold of him and with both of her hands wrapped around him there was still three or four inches of cock showing. Kathy pulled him toward her and her tongue flicked out and licked his cockhead and then she opened her mouth. Her mouth was barely able to get the cockhead in, but she tried her best and eventually she managed to get two or three inches in. That large cock sticking in that small mouth, lips stretched almost to the point of tearing the skin, coupled with the look of pure lust on Kathy's face was almost obscene. But it was also one of the most exciting things I had ever seen and my cock told me that it knew what I was thinking. Kathy tried to do for several minutes what was obvious to me that she couldn't - give her stud a blowjob - before she finally admitted to herself that she was wasting her time and took her mouth off him.

By that point I had undergone a major change in attitude and I was no longer reluctant to see or hear what was going to be happening in the master bedroom. I closed the door and climbed out the den window and made a run for the back door. If I could get into the house and to the staircase before Kathy got out of the chair to lead him upstairs I could beat them to the bedroom and get into the closet. Luck was with me, but only barely. I could hear them at the bottom of the stairs just as I went through the bedroom door. From the look of lust I had seen on Kathy's face I doubted if I was going to get a call for help, unless it was to help hold her down while her dancer tried to get it all in. They were in the room before I had a chance to get settled in and Kathy wasted no time in dragging the dancer over to the bed. She stripped in record time and threw herself down on the bed - no foreplay here - she wanted that cock and she wanted it now. That is, she did until he tried to get it in. I saw her face contort with pain as the head of the dancer's cock split her pussy lips and I expected to hear her say stop at any minute, but I saw her clench her jaw and will her body to accept the huge intruder. He managed to get about three inches in before she told him to stop and pull out.

"I need some lube baby. I've never had anything that big in me before."

She got the tube of K-Y that we use whenever she wants to be fucked in her ass and poured some on the dancer's cock. The three inches went back in fairly quickly, but then I saw her face contort again. "Easy baby, easy. I'm just a little girl and you got to be slow and easy with me."

This was probably nothing new for him and he went very slow, with short half-inch strokes, stopping every seven or eight strokes to put on some more K-Y. Slowly, but surely, his massive pole was disappearing from sight. It took him almost ten minutes to get it all in, but finally he was buried in Kathy to the root. Slowly he started working his dick in and out, first short strokes and then gradually they became longer and longer until he was pulling nine or ten inches out before sliding all the way back in. The look on Kathy's face was one of pure lust. For several minutes he fucked her slow and easy and then I heard the "ohohohohoh" that signaled Kathy's orgasm, but it was unlike any orgasm I'd seen her have before. Her body shook and thrashed around and I'm surprised that she didn't buck him off and then she fell back limp with a glazed look in her eyes. The dancer hadn't cum yet and he kept fucking Kathy's limp body, but the strokes were picking up in tempo. Suddenly Kathy's legs came up and locked behind the dancer's; her hands came up and grabbed his butt and she started moaning, "oh yes, oh yes, oh yes, fuck me, fuck me, fuck me," the words all running together as one depraved sexual sound. The dancer was driving hard now and Kathy was holding on for dear life. He said something in her ear and she moaned, "Not yet baby, not yet. I'm almost there, please wait, please wait, please baby," and then she screamed as she had one massive orgasm at the same time that the dancer drove home and held himself in her while his balls drained.

The two of them lay there on the bed, breathing hard and not moving, the dancer still buried to the hilt in Kathy's pussy. I became aware of a warm stickiness in my hand and looked down to see that I had cum all over the front of my pants and the inside of the closet door. I had been so wrapped up in the scene playing out in front of me that I hadn't been aware that I'd been stroking myself, let alone that I'd gotten myself off.

A low moan pulled my attention back to the bed and I saw Kathy looking up at the dancer with a look of astonishment on her face. The reason became clear to me when the dancer lifted himself up and then drove back down into Kathy; he either had not lost his hard on or he had hardened again while lying on top of her. She had adjusted to his size by now and she was full of both their fluids for lubrication so there were no more cries of "take it easy on me" and the dancer started to fuck Kathy hard and fast. I watched as she went crazy with lust and desire; she begged and pleaded with him to fuck her harder and faster, that he never stop, and she had orgasm after orgasm as the dancer tried to get himself off again. When he finally reached his goal and pumped his second load of the night into her, Kathy looked like a limp rag doll.

When he pulled out of her one last spurt of cum came out of the head of his dick and splashed on her stomach, and then he did something totally unexpected, he switched positions and went down on Kathy, licking his own juices out of her cunt. His limp dick was dangling just above Kathy's face and a small drop of cum fell on the tip of her nose and she opened her eyes to see the cock hanging over her mouth. Her tongue flicked out and licked the head of the dancer's cock and that was the signal he had been waiting for. He lowered himself and several inches of his cock disappeared into Kathy's mouth. Since he was now soft she was able to get more of him into her mouth than the first time she tried, but even soft it was still huge. I wished I had a camera to take a picture of the scene; Kathy's hands in the dancer's hair pulling his face into her cunt and with that huge log in her tiny mouth. Kathy's eyes suddenly got big as he began to get hard again. She pulled her head back to let some of it out, but the dancer pushed down to get it back in and he started to fuck Kathy's mouth. Her hands left his hair and she tried to push him away, but the dancer continued to stroke in and out of her mouth. I could see panic in her eyes as the monster cock started choking her and I started to reach for the door to go out and pull him off of her. But just as my hand touched the knob the dancer switched positions and drove his cock all the way into Kathy with one hard push. Kathy gave a loud grunt as the dancer bottomed out, he started to fuck her hard and fast and her arms and legs came up and gripped him.

I lost count of how many times Kathy came before the dancer exploded in Kathy for the third time that night. When the dancer pulled out and got off the bed I could see the gaping hole between Kathy's legs and I'd swear that if I was keeling in front of her with a flashlight I could have looked up that tunnel and counted her teeth.

At this point I'm supposed to tell about how the dancer left and Kathy thanked me for letting her have the experience of her life and then we lived happily ever after, but you wouldn't believe me, and you would be right. There is more of this story to come.

***

When the dancer pulled his cock out of Kathy's cunt and got off the bed I could see the gaping hole between her legs and I'd swear that if I was kneeling in front of her with a flashlight I could have looked up that tunnel and counted her teeth. I watched as it slowly closed, squeezing out a glob of cum as it did. Kathy lay spent on the bed and watched as the dancer got dressed. What happened next I would not have seen had I been in the guestroom where I was supposed to be. The dancer finished dressing and when he was ready to leave Kathy sat up and asked, "Can I see you again?"

That brought me up short because this was only supposed to be a 'one time' thing. The dancer took a piece of paper and a pen from his shirt pocket, wrote something on the paper and handed it to Kathy, "Anytime you want sweetie, just give me a call."

I watched as she put it in the top drawer of the bedside table and then got up to walk the dancer to the front door. As soon as they were out of the bedroom I made a mad dash to the bathroom to get a towel to clean up the mess I'd made in the closet. Then I took a quick look at the paper that Kathy had put in the top drawer, "Terry 555-1675" and then I hurried down to the guest bedroom. I was sitting on the bed when Kathy came into the room, still naked, and with cum running down her inner thighs.

"I didn't hear any calls for help so I guess everything went okay?"

Kathy shrugged and said, "It was okay, nothing special, just okay."

I put my book down and said, "So what school of thought do you belong to now, bigger is better, or knowing how to use it?"

Kathy was silent for a moment and then said; "Bigger isn't all that it's cracked up to be. I think I much prefer the "knowing how to use it"."

"Does that mean I don't have to get you the same present for Christmas, Valentine's Day, or our anniversary?"

She smiled at me and lied through her teeth, "No baby, once was enough."

I reached up and took hold of her arms and pulled her down to me, "Let's see if I can still touch the sides."

Kathy squealed and tried to pull away from me, "Don't baby, his cum is still inside me."

"Yeah, I know," I said as I slid into her. I was surprised that, even though extremely wet and sloppy, I could still feel the walls of her pussy and I was equally surprised at how deliciously wicked and wanton it felt to be soaking my cock in another man's cum. I thought that I could learn to like it, that and watching.

***

When I woke up the next morning it was with the realization that my marriage to Kathy was going to undergo some major changes. It was obvious to me, regardless of what Kathy had said the other evening about "once being enough", that she fully intended to treat herself to more of Terry's dick. What's more, she intended to do it behind my back. I don't know how she expected to hide it from me since we have sex five or six times a week and there is no way I wouldn't know what she'd been doing once I slid my dick in her. The only way she could hide it would be to cut me off altogether and that in itself would make me suspicious. I suppose that I could have made things easier by just telling her that I had been in the closet, that I had gotten turned on watching, and that I had loved sliding into the sloppy mess her dancer had left in her. But I didn't, probably because I was pissed that she was getting ready to go behind my back and that just didn't seem right considering what I had voluntarily allowed her to do.

It was stupid not to tell her because I was cutting off my nose to spite my face. After all, I wanted to watch and it would have been a whole lot easier if we were in it together. Instead, I'd put myself into a position where I would never know where or when and any chance that I would have to watch was going to be hit or miss. Oh well, I never claimed to be a genius. Since I was determined to watch and not let Kathy know that I knew she was cheating on me, I set out to find ways of doing it. I began searching the local library for "how to" information and I discovered how to wire a voice activated tape recorder to my telephone system and I also put one in our bedroom. It took the better part of a week and a half to find the info and buy the recorders (and they aren't cheap) and six times during that period I was aware of getting sloppy seconds from Kathy. Her excuse for being so wet was, "I've been constantly horny since my birthday and so I'm always wet and ready for you."

Yeah! Right! And the looseness?

***

I got home from work on the first day the tape recorders were in operation and went straight to my basement workshop. I played the tape that was hooked up to the phones and heard Kathy make a date with Terry for two in the afternoon at our house. Kathy was out someplace so I ran up to the bedroom and got the tape out of the recorder and took it back to the basement to listen to it. I listened to the sounds of flesh smacking flesh while Kathy begged her dancer to fuck her harder, to fuck her faster, and to push it in deeper. She moaned, she groaned and she screamed as her dancer fucked her for hours, but I didn't hear it all because the tape was only ninety minutes long. What I heard was enough to give me a hard on and I met Kathy when she came in the front door and fucked her right there on the floor.

"Jesus," she said, "What got into you?"

"Nothing much," I said, "I just keep thinking of you with that dancer's big cock in you and it gets to me sometimes."

There you go Kathy, I thought, your golden opportunity to bring me in, but she didn't say a word. For the next week it was pretty much the same. Come home, play the tapes, and fuck Kathy like a sex fiend on the days she fucked Terry. I got no useful information from the tapes because Terry always stayed longer than the tapes ran. Apparently they made their plans before he left so I never heard them. And then one day I got lucky. It was a Thursday afternoon and I had taken half a day off from work. Thursday was Kathy's day for her regular appointment at the hairdressers so she wasn't home when I got there. I was in the basement workshop working on a gun rack I was building when the phone rang and I picked up the phone, but before I could say hello I heard Kathy say it. She had come in and I hadn't heard her, and we both must have picked up at the same time.

"Kathy? This is Margo."

I started to put the phone down when two things happened simultaneously, I heard the word "Terry" and I suddenly realized that if I put the phone down Kathy would hear the click and know I was home. She must have parked in the drive and come in the front door which would have kept her from seeing my car in the garage. I put the phone back to my ear and heard "coming over this afternoon?" Kathy said yes, that he would be here about two.

Margo said, "I need a favor. Can I use your spare bedroom this afternoon? Dennis has the plumbers coming over this afternoon and I had already planned on spending the afternoon with Randy. I'm desperate, I haven't been laid in a week!"

Kathy laughed and said, "God, I wouldn't want to be responsible for making you go one more day without a dick. Come on over. I'll run to the store and get some stuff and we'll have a little party."

Margo said, "Thanks girlfriend, you're a lifesaver."

I heard the click when Kathy hung up and I put my phone back on the hook and crept to the top of the basement stairs. I waited till I heard the front door close and then I hurried to the front window so I could watch Kathy leave and then I ran out to the garage, got in my car and moved the car a block over from our house. I ran back to the house and got myself upstairs and into the closet. My watch said two twenty-five so I had at least a half-hour wait until Terry arrived. As it worked out I didn't have to wait that long; Kathy was back by two-forty, Terry rang the bell at two-fifty and by two fifty-five they were naked on the bed and fucking up a storm.

I could not believe how sexually exciting it could be for me to watch my wife being pounded by another man and cock size had nothing to do with it. I knew I would love watching any cock disappear into her hot box. I had my cock in my hand and I was slowly stroking it when Margo appeared in the doorway. She stood there until Kathy noticed her and then Margo gave a little "just letting you know I'm here" wave and disappeared down the hall. I felt a small bit of disappointment that I wasn't in the spare bedroom closet because I would have loved to see Margo with her clothes off. She was five feet tall, weighed maybe a hundred pounds, had flaming red hair and 36C cup tits and every guy that knew her wanted to fuck her (including me), but she always gave every indication that she was completely faithful to her husband.

An hour later I was still stroking my dick and watching Kathy have orgasm after orgasm as Terry fucked her, ate her and fucked her again. I was concentrating on the sight of Terry's massive cock disappearing into Kathy's cunt when Margo came back into the room. She was naked and looked every bit as glorious as I'd thought she would, and she was holding hands with a guy who was as naked as she was. He was maybe two inches taller than Margo, but his cock was every bit as big as Terry's, if not just a tad bigger. The two of them stood there and watched Terry put the pipe to Kathy until he finally pulled his shrinking cock out of her. He collapsed after pumping his fourth load of the afternoon into Kathy and I just knew he was done. I didn't see how he could possibly get it up again without resting for an hour or so.

Margo said, "You want to switch for a while?"

Kathy held out her arms to Margo's stud, and he went right to work. Margo got onto the bed next to Terry and took his limp cock in her mouth and I'll be damned if she didn't get him back up in less than two minutes. Margo's guy fucked Kathy twice, and I can't even begin to describe how weird it was to watch this five foot two guy with an eleven-inch cock fucking my five foot eight inch wife. Kathy finally called a halt to things, "Hubby will be home pretty soon and I need to clean the place up and douche myself, just in case he wants to get laid tonight."

Terry said, "Same time next week? I could bring a couple of friends if you want."

Kathy looked at Margo and the two of them nodded at each other and then Kathy said, "Yes, but let's get started earlier, say eleven-thirty?"

As soon as I heard them all at the front door, I quietly went down the stairs and then out the back door. I ran for my car and raced back to the house, getting there just as Margo was backing out the drive. She saw me and waved and I waved back and then I raced for the front door. The last thing I wanted was for Kathy to get a chance to clean herself up before I could get my cock in her. I dashed in the front door and into the living room just in time to see her going up the stairs. She turned, startled by my sudden appearance, "What are you doing home so early?"

I told her, truthfully, that I had been thinking of nothing else since two o'clock, but "Getting my cock into your hot wet pussy."

She glanced quickly upstairs and then back at me (can't have him go upstairs and see the cum stained sheets) and then she turned and came back down the steps. I took her right there on the floor and this time I could barely feel the walls of her pussy, but god did I love that hot wet feeling as my cock soaked in the juices of her two lovers. That night I gave her another chance at not having to cheat on me.

"You know why I was so hot to get home and fuck you today? It's because I can't get the image of you and your big cocked dancer out of my mind. I'm sorry now that I didn't stay in the room with you when you fucked him, or at least have been in the closet. You want to try him again with me around?"

She nodded her head no, "No thanks baby. I told you once was enough. I'm completely happy with you."

Yeah! Right! Lying bitch.

***

The following Tuesday I was in the closet when the guests started to arrive. First it was Margo and then five minutes later Randy showed up. Ten minutes after that Terry came in with three guys. I won't go into the discomfort that I suffered from hiding in the house for five hours until everybody got there. I'd kissed Kathy goodbye that morning and told her I would probably have to work late that night and then I left for work. I parked one block over and then I snuck back to the garage and waited until I heard Kathy taking her morning shower. I ran upstairs to the guestroom and then waited. When I heard the doorbell five hours later I headed for the closet in the master bedroom.

I watched five straight hours of Kathy and Margo being fucked steadily by the five guys. The two women were never without a cock in at least one of their holes the entire time. I came twice on the inside of the closet door and was stroking myself hard again when suddenly I heard Kathy say, "In the closet," to something that Margo had asked. Margo got off the bed and headed straight for my hiding place. I was fucked! The door opened, Margo saw me and stepped back in surprise. Impulsively or instinctively, I'm not sure which, I put my finger to my lips and hoped she would be quiet. The look on Margo's face went from surprise to wicked smile and she winked at me. She bent down to pick up a pair of Kathy's high heels (I found out later that she wanted them so she could stand next to the bed and get fucked from behind. Apparently the heels gave her just the right angle for better penetration) and as her face passed my hard on got she stopped long enough to lick the head and then kiss it. As she straightened up she mouthed the words "later," and went back to the orgy taking place on the bed. I did not get to Kathy that night - she would not let me near her. She claimed backaches, stomachaches and headaches and she spent an hour soaking in a hot tub of water. She knew that if I'd fucked her after her gangbang I'd be sure to know what she was up to.

The next day Margo called me at work and asked me to have lunch with her. She got right to the point, "How long have you known?"

From the very beginning I told her and she gave me a questioning look and so I told her everything from the birthday present, to the way I felt when I fucked Kathy after her lovers, to yesterday's orgy. I told her about my frustration at not knowing when things were going to happen so I could be there to watch and she reached across the table and patted my hand, "Poor baby. We will have to do something about that. I'll help, but there is a price."

"What?" I asked. "You will have to let me suck your dick."

We spent the afternoon at a motel and it was marvelous. Margo's plan was simplicity itself. Her husband Dennis knew about her affairs and he didn't care. Margo would convince Kathy that it would be better to meet Terry (or whomever) at Margo's as that would eliminate any possibility of my coming home some day and catching her. Then Margo would tell me when and what time and I could be there in time to watch, and that's just what we have done.

For the last six months now I've watched Kathy and Margo fuck at least thirty-five different guys; sometimes only one guy and sometimes in groups as large as ten and I never get tired of seeing those cocks pounding into Kathy's cunt. The down side is that about fifty percent of the time I can never get home in time to soak my cock in her cum filled cunt; she manages to be cleaned up by the time I get there. However there is an upside to the downside. The reason I can't get home in time is because Margo is on me as soon as I come out of the closet, and she has added a whole dimension to things. She sits on my face and has me eat her out. I don't know why I've never done it with Kathy - it's just as depraved as wanting to soak my cock in Kathy's cum filled cunt, and I've come to love it.

I've burned up most of my sick time, personal days and vacation time in Margo's closet and I'm about to the point where I am going to have to let Kathy know that I'm aware of her cheating. We need to schedule things for the evenings when I can be home, but I really don't want to. It is such a turn on to watch her and to know that she doesn't know that I know, and then of course there is Margo. I'm not sure that Kathy would approve of that, but then no one ever said life was going to be fair.

The End

Here is a sample from another story you may enjoy:

BLACKMAILED

MILF

LUSTY MOTHER SEDUCTION

JUST PLAIN BOB

Ralph was gone on his trip and Patty was staying the night with a girlfriend and She didn't feel like sitting at home and watching TV or staring at the walls. She looked in the paper and found a movie that She would like to see so She went upstairs, took a shower and got dressed. She debated on whether to wear a skirt or slacks and decided on a skirt. At the last minute She also decided to wear heels. Ralph didn't seem to care anymore, but maybe She could get a wolf whistle or two to pump up her ego.

She was driving down Grant Street when She saw a flashing sign that said, "Live music, 7 till 1:30." And on a whim She pulled into the parking lot and had gone inside. The band was playing Seventies rock and roll and She decided that sitting and listening to the music and having a few drinks would do her a lot more good than popcorn, a soft drink and a movie. She found an empty table and ordered a drink and before the cocktail waitress got back with her vodka tonic She had been asked to dance twice. She politely refused – She wasn't there trolling for a man – She was just there to relax and listen to the music.

By the time She had finished her fourth drink her body was swaying to the music and her foot was tapping to the beat and when the next man asked her to dance She said yes. Talk about an ego stroke, the guy wasn't much older than Patty. She couldn't interest her own husband, but a young stud half her age didn't mind holding her close and pushing an erection into her leg and belly. She didn't lead him on, but She didn't push him away either. It felt good to be desired, especially after months of being ignored by Ralph.

She let the young man, Dirk, join her at her table and buy her another drink, and then another and by the time last call came She was feeling no pain. She was also horny as hell and hot enough to fuck from Dirk's hard cock being pressed into her every time they danced. Even though She'd had a lot more to drink than was good for her She still had enough presence of mind to deflect Dirk's advances.

"Sorry baby, but I'm not looking for that. I'm just a married woman who didn't want to stay home alone tonight. I just came in here for a couple of drinks and to listen to the music."

Dirk kept trying, but he wasn't pushy about it and he seemed to accept that as far as She was concerned getting to her was a lost cause. That is he accepted it until the bar closed and it was time to leave. Dirk had walked her to her car and when She had turned to say goodnight he had taken her in his arms and kissed her. She knew She should have pushed him away and She actually had her hands against his chest to do it when he slipped his tongue into her mouth. It felt so good to be kissed with a little passion and besides, what harm could a little kiss do? She had returned the kiss with a little tongue of her own and when the kiss ended She had felt a little giddy.

She had turned away from him, her loins on fire and knowing that she would regret passing up the opportunity, and bent to unlock her car door. She dropped her keys and Dirk had picked them up and given them back to her and she had dropped them a second time. He picked them up again and handed them to her saying, "Want me to do it?"

"Don't be silly. I'm perfectly capable of..." and She dropped them again.

"That does it sweetie, I'm not letting you drive home in that condition" and he had overruled her protests as he got her in the car and then got in on the driver's side.

***

The first picture had appeared two days later. She had come down to the kitchen to put on the coffee and when She had gone to the refrigerator for the cream She found it stuck to the door with a small refrigerator magnet. It showed her on her hands and knees, a look of pure lust on her face and Dirk taking her from behind. Where had it come from? Who had taken it? She had been alone in the house with Dirk, Ralph wasn't due back for two more days and Patty had been staying at Shelly's. God, She had known that giving in to Dirk was a mistake, a highly enjoyable mistake, but a mistake none the less.

The second picture was in the mailbox that day with the regular mail. It was in a plain white envelope addressed simply "To The Slut." It showed her on her hands and knees sucking Dirk's cock. No note, no comment on the back of the photo to indicate who had taken the picture or what they were after. One thing was for sure though, that there were more and maybe a lot more. The pictures were on standard copy and computer paper and had obviously been captured from videotape.

She had spent a nervous day waiting for the phone to ring or someone to knock on the door and tell her what they were after, but nothing happened. She hadn't gotten much sleep that night either. The third picture was taped to the outside of her kitchen window and She saw it when She went to rinse out her coffee cup. She was naked, legs spread wide and her high heels pointing straight up at the ceiling as Dirk drove his cock deep into her pussy. She started to worry, no, panic is what She was feeling. Ralph would be home the next day and if whoever was doing this didn't make themselves known and reveal what they were after before he got home he might be the one finding the pictures and that would be disastrous. Granted, She and Ralph were not getting along all that well right then, but She did love him and didn't want to lose him. She kicked herself mentally for not thinking of that before letting Dirk into her bedroom.

***

The day had been long and worrisome. She had run to the phone every time it rang, afraid of who the caller might be and what they might want, but at the same time desperate to know. The only calls She got were the ones She normally got and the only one to knock on the door was a Jehovah's Witness. At three that afternoon She went out to get the mail and found a plain white box sitting on top of the bills and flyers. No postage or return address and like the envelope of the previous day it was addressed "To The Slut." She had broken a fingernail in her haste to open the box and inside She had found a note taped to the cartridge:

"Wear your shortest skirt, your lowest cut blouse and your highest heels. All will be revealed at seven tonight. Make sure that you do it because if you don't, guess who will be the next one to see a copy of the tape or find a picture stuck on the refrigerator."

The tape didn't have it all. It recorded the last three hours, but did not show the first forty-five minutes. Whoever shot the tape missed Dirk eating her pussy, the first fuck and the sixty-nine that followed, but they had gotten all the rest. In living color they had gotten all of the cock sucking, fucking and they had caught her screaming in pleasure as Dirk had sent his meaty cock as deep into her ass as it would go. Every "Fuck me harder" came through loud and clear. Every "That's it lover, just like that" and "Deep baby, push it deep" had the clarity of a ringing bell. The tape had ended on something that was almost worse than the illicit sex. In response to Dirk's "When can I see you again" She had said, "Let me see how I feel about this in the morning. Leave me your phone number."

Ralph could not see that tape. No matter what She had to do, Ralph could never ever see that tape.

If you enjoyed this sample, look for **Blackmailed MILF**.

Also by this Author:

From the Author

If you enjoyed any of my books then please share the love and promote my books in Amazon.

If you write me a review and send me an email I will send you a free book, or many.
(Just know that these emails are filtered by my publisher.)

Good news is always welcome.

One Last Thing, For Kindle Readers...

When you turn the page, Kindle will give you the opportunity to rate this book and share your thoughts on Facebook and Twitter. If you enjoyed my writings, would you please take a few seconds to let your friends know about it? Because... when they enjoy they will be grateful to you and so will I.

Thank You!

An Open Letter from Just Plain Bob

A message for those who like my stories, those who hate my stories, those who are indifferent and those who have yet to make up their minds.

I have often stated that I really don't care what others think about my stories, that I write for my own enjoyment and then I offer to share. If you like my stories fine and if you don't, also fine since I have already satisfied my target audience - me!

It is human nature to strive to get better. If you take up bowling your first games are going low scoring, but you will work and practice to get better and as your average climbs you may forget the game where you had three gutter balls and shot an eighty-six, but that game is still there in your past.

Your first time on the golf course you shot an eighty on the front nine, but did you settle for that being your game or did you work to improve? You may eventually get a three handicap, but that nine hole eighty is still there as part of your past.

When you hired in at your job did you say, "Cool, I got it made" and do nothing more than what you barely had to do or did you go to work thinking that, "Someday I'm going to be running this place." You might never climb that high, but human nature says that you are going to at least try.

It is the same with authors who write stories and post them on sites like Literotica. Their first stories might not be all that good, but comments and feedback along with a desire to get better drive them toward putting out a better product or to at least try.

I'm no different. My first stories might not have been all that great, but they are still there on the hard drive. I like cheating wife stories and five years ago I found my first adult site that catered to cheating wife stories. It was a pay site, but it had a policy of giving a free lifetime membership to anyone who submitted five stories to the site. How hard can that be I said to myself as I sat down and fired up the word processor and went to work.

I sent my five stories in and sat back to enjoy my free membership and a funny thing happened. I started getting feedback, most of it positive, and I became hooked. I started cranking out more stories. The site I was sending my stories to had seven categories:

Bisexual
Cream Pie

Groups
I Watch
Gang Bang
Racial
SM/BD

I know nothing about bisexual or SM/BD and I had no interest in Groups so all the stories I wrote I tailored for the four remaining categories:

Cream Pie
I Watch
Gang Bang
Racial.

I turned out eight stories a month, two for each category, which means that after five years I have over 120 stories in each of those categories and they are all still on the hard drive.

A year ago I received an email asking me why I never posted stories on Literotica. The answer? I didn't know about Lit. I pulled it up, liked what I saw, and started sending in stories to it. All new stories? No, not hardly, not with over 400 stories sitting on the hard drive. Maybe one new story for each fifteen or so old ones. The newer ones are better, at least I think they are and I have received some feedback that leads me to believe that others think so too, and I will continue to write new ones.

But I am still going to recycle what is on the hard drive, stories that were written specifically to fit the four categories. That means that those of you who hate cream pie stories still have eighty or so to look forward to. Ditto for those who call me a racist; you will get another seventy or so interracial stories.

Those who hate wimps will only see about fifty more of those because the stories I sent to the I Watch category were split 50/50 between what some call wimps and some call "real men." Why the 50/50 split? It came from listening to the readers. I would get feedback asking me why all the men in my stories were hard asses. "In real life men are more forgiving, especially if it is the first indiscretion." So I would write stories with forgiving husbands and boyfriends and then the next batch of feedback would say, "Why are all your husbands spineless wimps" and I'd write stories that went back the other way.

Eventually I came to realize that I was wasting my time - there was no way I could write a story that would satisfy everybody and that is when I adopted my philosophy of writing for my own enjoyment and then offering to share.

As far as the gangbang stories? Well, what can I say? Gangbangs are gangbangs and there are still eighty or so of them to go.

The bottom line is that Literotica readers are going to see more of my old stories than my new ones. If I'm still around three or four years from now it will probably go the other way, more new than old.

I feel the need to respond to some of the comments and emails I have received. By far the largest percentage comes from people who say, "You are an asshole because all women are not whores and sluts and that's all you make them out to be."

Next most common is, "You must really hate women you sick fuck."

"You must be a wimp because all the men in your stories are wimps" is up there in the top ten along with, "Why don't you give it a rest and go crawl off in a hole somewhere."

There is a lot more, but I'm only going to address those four and in reverse order.

I won't stop and go crawl in a hole because I am enjoying the hell out of what I am doing and remember what I said, I am doing this for MY OWN ENJOYMENT and then I offer to share. Some obviously like my sharing with them and so I will continue to do so. No one is holding a gun to a reader's head and telling them they must click on a Just Plain Bob story or die. It is a conscious choice on the reader's part to move that mouse and click on that story.

When a man finds out he has a cheating wife or girlfriend there are only a limited number of ways he can handle it. If he loves her he can forgive, try to forget and try to hold on and somehow make things work. He can turn his back on her, walk away and get on with his life. The third option is to take revenge.

According to a good portion of those who send me feedback the first and second options are proof that the men are wimps. If the man takes the third option he is still considered a wimp if he doesn't do some sort of physical damage to the woman and her lover. These readers believe that the only way not to be a wimp is to kill, maim and destroy everything in sight. Doing that however, will invariably get the man throw in jail and that is why it so rarely happens in real life.

In real life most revenge takes place in the man's head when he says to himself, "I should have _____ (fill in the blank) the fucking cunt!" I know this because I have been there and done that (see The Dark Trilogy). In my stories I try to mirror real life so kill, maim and destroy are going to be for the most part absent. Outside of some fisticuffs there will be very little physical violence in my stories. Most of my husbands are going to do what I did, what several of my friends and others that I know have done, forgive, or walk away. If this makes them wimps and me a wimp for writing the story that way, so be it.

Next is the "I must hate all women." Nothing could be farther from the truth. I love women. I lust after women. I even like whores and sluts. I have been married four times, engaged two other times (that did not end in marriage) and I have always had girlfriends between marriages. My philosophy is that women were put on this earth for me to enjoy and I'm not talking just sexually. I could sit at the mall (and have) for hours and just girl watch.

The engagements, girlfriends and three of the four marriages bring me to the #1 anti JPB comment on the list.

"You are an asshole because all women aren't whores and sluts."

Well dear reader, you can not prove that by me! I will say up front that I KNOW all women aren't whores and sluts, BUT the majority of the women in my life were. My mother ran around on my father for years while he was driving a truck for a living. My Aunt Margaret cheated regularly on my Uncle Bill, as did my Aunt Mildred on my Uncle Paul. My Aunt Betty fucked around on my Uncle Bob for years and finally left him for his brother, my Uncle Wendell. Uncle Wendell in turn caught her on her knees at his company Christmas party giving Season's Greetings to his boss.

My sister is three times divorced and each divorce came about when the then current husband caught her out spreading pollen. Both of the engagements I mentioned ended when I found out that I was not the one and only and a lot of the girls I dated between marriages never made it to engagement status for the same reason.

And that brings me to my three ex-wives. The first one, Helen (I believe I commented on her in the intro to The Dark Trilogy) had seven different lovers before I found out what was going on. I was living proof that love is blind. Ditto with my second wife. She had a secret life that she hid from me and when I found out about her brother, his friends and the gangbangs she was history.

My third marriage ended in divorce because of a different kind of cheating (and I can just imagine the outrage I am going to get over this) - she cheated on me with an idea. I was away from home on business, she was lonely, a couple of Jehovah's Witnesses knocked on the door and my wife, with nothing better to do invited them in. When I came home from my trip I found out that she had found God. On a scale that runs from TRUE BELIEVER on one end to ATHEIST on the other you will find me just to the right of AGNOSTIC and since I would not allow myself to be SAVED the marriage eventually died.

So yes, I write about sluts and whores because as everyone knows, you tend to write about the things you know. And I do like sluts and whores, just not the ones that lie to me and cheat on me.

So be forewarned - if you click on a Just Plain Bob story you will be getting sluts, whores and husbands who do not kill, maim and destroy. There are other things you will rarely find in a Just Plain Bob story. Even though I try to mirror real life my stories all take place in StoryLand. In StoryLand STDs and unwanted pregnancies do not exist unless the author feels like they may add something to the story. Bad things do not happen in StoryLand unless the author so wills it and no amount of "You should have..." in comments and feedback will change a story already posted.

Lastly, I will touch on a truth. None of what I have written here means shit because the same readers will still read the same stories that they profess to hate and make the same comments they have always made. Knowing this, I will deliberately post stories that will have them frothing at the mouth.

It is the least I can do for an adoring public.

Thank you!

Just Plain Bob
justplainbob@awesomeauthors.org